KAOS

Kick Ass Operatives Service

Nicky Testaforte

Testaforte Books

Chapter One

Aluminum bleachers surround an MMA cage in a dark, cramped building. Rowdy locals chug beers, scream, shout and pump their fists at the action in the cage.

Holly Prince, thick in a muscular yet feminine way, pummels Jen Lane. She's overwhelmed and retreats to the side of the cage.

Karla Rockoff, Holly's teammate screams.

"She's breaking."

Jen can't hide her panic as Holly headlocks her for a head and arm throw. Jen blatantly grabs the cage. The ref misses this as he moves to get a better view.

Jen falls on top of Holly after the cage grab.

"She grabbed the cage, ref," Karla screams.

Holly is in a precarious spot. Jen's demeanor goes from lost to confident and determined. She's mounted Holly and rains down punches and elbows.

The situation is escalating but Holly is calm and composed on her back. She moves her head from side to side and uses her arms to dodge and block most of the blows.

A punch gets through. It slices open Holly's left eyebrow.

"You know what to do here girl," Karla screams.

Jen frantically swings her fists and elbows at Holly's head. The Ref leans in.

Do something Holly, or I'll be forced…" says the Ref.

He can't finish his statement as Holly quickly climbs her feet up the cage and pushes off.

Jen lunges forward a bit. Holly is flexible and fast enough to slip out from under her before she can change positions.

In one fluid motion, Holly simultaneously wraps her legs around Jen's head and into a triangle choke, rolls her over, and ends up on top.

Holly smashes Jen's nose and then tightens the choke, causing a tap. The crowd roars as Holly releases the hold.

Karla and the trainer raise their arms and celebrate. Still on her knees, Holly bows and shows respect to her opponent. The ref looks at Jen's mangled face and yells.

"We need the doctor in here."

The trainer rushes in and hugs Holly. Karla's cheery face turns serious as she approaches.

"What took so long? I would've smashed that girl in ten seconds."

"Maybe, but your body is breaking down and you're too scared to get into the cage these days."

"This body is perfect. The only thing I fear is one day looking like you do in a dress."

The fight doctor approaches Holly. Karla briefly locks eyes with him and turns back to Holly.

"And what was up with that botched throw?"

"Are you serious? She grabbed the cage!"

"All I saw was bad technique."

Karla looks on as the trainer finishes tending to Holly's cut. Holly takes out her phone out of her duffel bag and dials a number.

"Hey honey, It's mommy. Calling to say I love you and miss you. I'll see you soon okay, buddy?"

Karla sees the fight doctor turn down a hallway. She follows him. The doctor looks around nervously as Karla approaches. Karla is carefree and smiling.

"Eh...What's up, doc?"

"You know, this is getting increasingly difficult for me and risky to my reputation."

"Aw, my hero."

"Enough, Karla."

The doctor looks around and then pulls a prescription pill bottle out of his bag.

"Here, ten-milligram oxy is all I could get."

"Ten? Last time it was twenty and I told you that crap gives me horror show nightmares and side effects."

"So you don't want them?"

"Did I say that? I'm not paying extra for a weaker pill."

"More risk, same price."

"You realize I could beat the crap out of you and just take them?"

"I don't dispute that. If those are the thoughts going through your head then you most definitely have a problem."

"It's a joke, doc."

Karla pulls out the money. They quickly exchange cash for pills. The doctor turns and walks away.

Karla enters the bathroom and looks in the mirror. She shakes out her right shoulder and then takes the pill bottle out. She tosses two pills in her mouth, swallowing them dry. She pulls a vitamin bottle out of her purse. She dumps the pills in, throws the pill bottle into the trash, and exits the bathroom.

As Karla comes out of the bathroom, Holly walks toward her with a towel over her head.

"Yo, towel head!"

"Not now, sister. I need a fistful of painkillers and a long hot shower.

Just as Karla is about to respond, her phone rings.

"It's Kane."

Holly grabs the phone from Karla and puts it on speaker.

"Who's this?"

"Very funny. I hope you've saved up your strength and didn't get too beat up."

"She looked beat up before she got into the ring."

Holly elbows Karla in the ribs.

"Did ya call just to chat, 'cause I'd like to stand under a hot shower till the water runs out?"

"If you did that, you'd melt like a candle."

Karla sways and gets smaller. "I'm melting, I'm melting."

"Ladies, We've got a job. Go home and pack a bag. You're going to Texas."

"For barbecue?" Holly says excitedly.

"No wonder you're so fat..."

"Settle down, ladies. I suggest you pack a couple of slinky dresses along with your rip stops."

"Ooh, a swanky job. Cool." Holly says.

"The jet leaves Teterboro tomorrow at 9 AM. Don't be late."

"Are ya sure she has to come?" Karla asks.

"Hey!"

"Oh, this one requires both of your specific charms," Kane says.

"She doesn't have any charms," Karla says.

"Enough sparring, ladies. Times ticking and Texas calls. Say goodbye."

Karla covers Holly's mouth and grabs the phone from her hands. Holly breaks loose, comes behind Karla and puts a choke hold on her

"Bye, Arty!" Karla gags.

Chapter Two

Holly walks downstairs, suitcase in hand. On the couch is her father and her ten-year-old autistic son Jeremy, who is rocking back and forth.

"Mommy go?" Says Jeremy.

"It's O.K., Jeremy. Grandpa is here with you."

Holly drops the suitcase, and heads to the couch kneeling in front of Jeremy. She takes his hand in hers.

"That's right, sweetie. Mommy is going on a plane. Grandpa will be here to take you to program just like Mommy does."

"Mommy stay?"

"Mommy has to go to work, Jeremy." Her dad says.

"Mommy stay...mommy stay?!"

'Mommy will be back sooner than you know it. And, I'll FaceTime with you every night before you go to bed."

"Now come and give Mommy big hug."

Jeremy gets up and gives Holly a weak hug, but she squeezes back tightly.

"Now, be good for Grandpa."

Jeremy pulls away and Holly raises a hand.

"High five?"

Jeremy responds with a hard slap.

"Low Five?"

Jeremy goes to slap her hand but Holly reaches out to tickle him and he begins to giggle and pull away.

"We'll be fine, Holly. You better get going. Say hello to Kane for me and tell that leatherneck he owes me a bottle of Macallan."

Holly gives her father a hug.

"I will. And don't forget, the speech therapist will be here tomorrow at 10AM."

As she leaves, she looks back and Jeremy is jumping up and down on his indoor trampoline, flapping his hands. She blows them a kiss and heads out.

* * *

A private jet idles on the tarmac. The stairs are down and from a distance, a muscle car is approaching quickly.

A black Shelby Cobra approaches the jet. The driver slides the car to a stop so it's facing the jet. Holly gets out, grabs her bag, and walks up the stairs of the jet. Halfway up, she hears a loud Harley approach and she smiles.

Tommy Stone comes into view and circles around next to the Cobra. He grabs a duffel from the back of the bike and heads toward the jet.

"Afternoon, sunshine. Didn't know you'd be joining us."

"When I heard Texas, I figured what the hell. You could use the help and I could use a fat, juicy steak."

"Is Karla coming?"

"Late as usual. Probably doing her makeup on the way over."

Both turn as sirens in the distance are getting closer and louder. A 69 Camaro SS appears, closely followed by a Police Cruiser with lights and sirens blaring.

"Oh how cute. She brought a welcoming committee."

"You better make the call."

"I'd rather make her squirm."

The Camaro stops just before the Cobra and the police car angles into it. As Karla gets out, the Cop approaches yelling at her.

"What the hell is your problem, lady? I clocked you doing sixty and that was just coming in here."

Batting her eyelashes and posing, Karla says sweetly "Sorry, officer. I was running late."

Holly approaches with a cell phone in her hand.

"Officer, it's for you."

The cop grabs the phone and listens.

"O.K....not a problem....yes, sir..."

The Officer kills the call and hands the phone back to Holly.

"You guys have friends in high places."

"Miss, please take it easy out there from now on?"

"Why certainly, Officer. I'm so sorry. Is there anything I can do for you?"

"Oh, brother. Leave it alone, will you? We gotta get going."

Holly pulls Karla toward the jet.

Tommy grabs a seat and begins surfing on his iPad. Holly and Karla enter talking.

"My god, woman. Do you fall for every guy in a uniform or what?"

"Nah, just the young and cute ones."

The front-mounted wide-screen monitor shows a split screen of Artemis Kane and hacker Javi Ordonez patiently waiting for the women to get seated, so they can begin the briefing.

When Karla sees Javi on screen, she yells out…

"Haveeee!! How are you, bud?"

"I'm good, K. No complaints."

"As soon as you ladies are settled in we can get this show on the road."

"All I need for this brunch meeting is a tall mimosa and a never-ending supply of caviar." Says Holly.

Karla throws a bottle of water at Holly. "Here's a bottle of water. Drown yourself in it. And I'm the one everybody considers high maintenance."

"O.K., kids. Our mark today is Sam Heatherwood. 3rd generation oilman and 1st generation tech angel.

"What the hell is a tech angel?" Holly asks.

"He invests his family's oil money in the tech sector. Seems that Sammy has rudely taken possession of a critical piece of our client's code and we need to get it back.”

“Can't you get it, Javi?”

“If it were that easy, I'd have it by now. He's taken a solid state hard drive and we know it's locked up in a safe on his yacht.”

“Mr. Heatherwood is having a gala on his yacht tonight and you're all invited...sort of.”

“What does that mean, Arty?”

“Heatherwood's a fan of MMA, so as a surprise to him...”

“Aw, great. Does this mean autographs and photo ops?” Karla asks.

“Let's hope that's kept to a dull roar because you're going to entice Heatherwood to his bedroom and get him to open the safe.”

"And that doesn't mean repeatedly bashing his head into it to get it to open. You gotta show some of that skin, sister." Holly says.

"Why can't Tommy do it?" Karla asks.

"If I show him some skin it's gonna be my fist to his mouth. You're much more subtle, Karla. So, Kane, who do I get to dress up and be?"

"Tommy in a dress. Sorry, can't picture that." Holly says.

"I want you to reach out to your SEAL buds because you're going to support the ladies when they get the drive in a waterproof pouch."

"What's so special about this data that we have to go in for it?"

"This drive not only has the specs for a super collider, it also has its operating system on it. Without this, it won't run, and now that Heatherwood has it, he could build his own."

"What does a supercollider do?" Holly asks.

"It bashes your head in like I do."

"More like you wish you could do."

"It's beyond my pay grade to attempt to describe it to you Holly." Javi, tell 'em what we have on Heatherwood."

"Sam Heatherwood, 45 years old, married father of four. Two 18-year-old twin boys Jake and Harry and two girls 10-year-old Allison and 15-year-old Melissa. Wife Gina Heatherwood is a full-time socialite who's conveniently out of the country on a shopping spree in Paris.

"What size is she?" Holly asks.

"Size?" Kane asks.

"Yeah, dress size. If she's buying more, I'll gladly take the socialite's sloppy seconds."

"I heard that's what you say when you're on the prowl. Give me your sloppy seconds."

"Anybody have some gaffers tape and a rag I can borrow?"

"I've got the gaffers tape."

"Hey, Tommy, who's side are you on?"

"Javi, please continue."

"The event will take place on his 165-foot yacht, The Seraphina.

"Jeez, look at that thing," Tommy says.

"I got me one of them boats. Mine has a helicopter." Karla says.

"Heatherwood's honoring Naveet Khan, the first female to successfully grow a company with a market cap of one billion dollars with funding from his Angel Investors Group."

"What does she make?" Holly asks.

"Not make, do. Her company provides internet access to third world countries and she gets a cut from any development resultant from that."

"Great. Now kids in mud huts can download porn." Holly says.

"Why do you always go gutter?"

"Well, that's where I found you."

"What does he have for security?" Tommy asks.

"His detail consists of former Special Forces operatives who will be dressed to the nines so they blend in with the crowd."

"Is that all?"

"A medical records search pulled up that Mr. Heatherwood has a life-threatening anaphylactic reaction to peanuts."

"Be a good boy, Sammy, and chew those peanuts for Aunt Karla now."

Karla makes loud choking sounds as she grabs her throat and convulses in the seat."

"Anything else?" Holly asks.

"Yeah, getting in will be easy. Getting out, not so much. Once they find out we have the drive, all hell is going to break loose."

"So I assume you ordered up four or five Apache helicopters with hellfire missiles to create a diversion, right?" Karla asks.

"We're well paid for this job, Karla, but not that well."

"So after we get the drive, how are we getting out?"

"I think you'll do alright."

"ARTY!!"

"Just kidding. Javi and I have a plan, we're just working it out. As soon as we nail it down, we'll let you know. Bye, kids."

Javi waves and the monitor goes black.

Chapter Three

Holly, Karla, and Tommy are seated in a curved booth before a spread of steaks, baked potatoes, and bottles of wine.

"This sure beats protein drinks," Tommy says.

"If I ate like this every night, I'd be a shoo-in for that show My 600 Pound Life," Karla says.

"Look at it this way, if you were that big, you could hide Twinkies in your rolls of fat," Holly says.

"Oh no."

"What, Ring Dings then?"

"No, Myron Speltz is making a beeline to our table and he's got company.

"Ah, crap. Lisa the Lioness." Holly mutters.

Speltz appears along with a large woman, Lisa Lee.

"Good evening, ladies. What brings you to my neck of the woods?"

"I think the tide washed them up," Lee says.

"Myron, you're interrupting a very important dinner with our long-lost cousin who happens to have a nasty aversion to slugs like you," Holly Says.

"Then what's he doing with you two urchins?" Lee says.

"Ladies, I'm in a little bit of a jam. The Lioness has a bout scheduled for tomorrow night but her opponent dropped out."

"Again," Lee says. "Bitch was afraid of me. They all are. What makes you think these two are any different Myron?"

"When I saw you two here, it was manna from heaven. I'm begging you. I need someone to take Lisa on or I'm gonna lose my shirt on this one. I'll make it worth your while." He rubs his fingers together.

"As tempted as I am to tame the Lioness..." Karla says.

"In your wildest dreams, twerp," Lee says.

"We have a prior engagement," Karla says

"With a reputable and well-paying gentleman of modest means," Holly says.

"So yous are hookers on the side too?" Lee says.

"Myron, I suggest you and your failed experiment turn heel and slither back into the hole you came from before I lose my patience," Tommy says.

Lisa starts to go after Tommy. Myron holds her back.

"Save it for the cage, honey."

Karla points a fork at her. "Yeah, down kitty."

"I wish you the best, Myron, but honestly, my steak is getting cold," Holly says.

Myron starts to head out. Lisa sneers at them.

"I won't forget this."

"I already did," Holly says.

Tommy gives them a below-the-chin wave.

"I just wanna eat in peace. Is that too much to ask?" Holly says.

"Nobody's stopping you from eating your peas, little girl."

"Funny...for a two-year-old."

“Don't turn around, but a guy has been staring at us since we got here. He's really setting off my radar.” Tommy says.

“Is he cute?” Karla asks.

“He's getting up now…and heading our way.”

“Nice.”

A large guy in a suit approaches the table.

“Hello, Holly.”

Holly drops her fork and her jaw. Face white, like she's seen a ghost.

“What the…”

“Let me explain.”

“Blackwater said…”

It finally hits Karla who the guy is. “Oh boy…”

“We mourned over an empty casket??.

“Tommy, Let's give them a minute,” Karla says.

"You O.K. here Holly?" Tommy says.

Karla just stares deadpan at the guy. Holly waves them off. Tommy sighs and gets up.

"What are you doing here with these people? Where's Jeremy? Did you guys move down here?"

"Where's Jeremy…Are you serious? You clearly abandoned us. So many nights I've had to sit there and explain to him where Daddy was. Let's not even talk about trying to raise a special needs son as a single mother."

"Give me a chance. I can explain everything, but I have a right to know how and where my son is."

"Jeremy's in the capable hands of my father."

"And how is the Commander these days?"

"If he knew you were alive, he'd be livid. He never trusted you and he was right all along. You need to leave. NOW."

"I've been keeping people like your father and our son safe from…"

"Someone else might fall for that line of crap, but not me. Maybe you believe it, but it's not the truth. That's just a lie you tell yourself. Derek, you were dead to me then, you're dead to me now."

Holly turns away.

"Fine. Enjoy your meal and be careful. I'll be seeing you, Holly."

He walks off. Holly angrily stabs at a piece of steak as Tommy and Karla return.

"You said he died in Afghanistan when he was over there with Blackwater. What did he say for himself?"

"Whatever he wanted to say, I'm not ready to hear it."

"Blackwater, huh? No wonder he set off my radar." Tommy says.

"Can we just drop this please?"

A young waiter approaches with a dessert menu in hand.

"Can I interest you in some dessert?"

"Are you on the menu?" Karla asks.

"Sorry, I'm gay."

"Nice to meet you, gay. I'm Karla"

"We'll take the check please."

"Very well."

"What do you say we settle up and go look at a boat?" Tommy says.

"You two go. I need to FaceTime with Jeremy."

"Tell that cutie that Aunt Karla says hi."

"You good Holly?" Tommy asks.

"I'm fine, go scope out the yacht."

Heatherwood's yacht is all lit up and abuzz with servants and crew setting up. As Karla and Tommy approach from the street, they hear footsteps behind them.

"Where's Holly?" Derek says.

"Are you following us?" Karla says.

"What are you people doing here?" Derek asks.

"Taking in the view with my best girl. What's your story?" Tommy says.

"Look, just tell Holly I want to explain everything."

"Do we look like an answering service? You tell her. Or just go back to playing dead again." Karla says.

"You might wanna teach this one some manners," Derek says.

Tommy steps up in his space.

"Don't talk to my girl like that."

Derek casually puts his hands up like he meant no harm.

"I'm done here. But just so you know, there are some really bad people around here. So I suggest you be careful in what you're doing."

"We can handle ourselves just fine. Now take it walking." Tommy says.

Derek turns and walks away. He pulls his cell phone out and makes a call.

★ ★ ★

Jeremy is at the dining room table drawing a detailed picture of someone with their arms raised in a "V" over an opponent.

Roger stands over him and smiles.

"Who's that, Jeremy?"

"Mommy TV."

The phone rings and Holly's father answers.

"Hello?"

"Hey, Dad."

"Holly, how's it going?"

Jeremy looks up from his drawing. "Mommy phone, mommy phone."

"Great. I want you to grab the iPad so Jeremy and I can FaceTime. But, first I have to tell you something."

"What is it?"

"I saw Derek today."

No reply from her father. There's silence on the line.

"Dad, are you still there?"

"I'm here...Did that son of a bitch give you an explanation on how he rose from the dead??"

"Dad, I...I just wanted him gone."

"I understand. But this raises even more questions. I'm gonna have to call in some favors to get to the bottom of this."

"I know, but before it gets too late, can you get Jeremy to FaceTime with me?

"He's right here, waiting."

"Dad, don't get too worked up about this."

"Too late, honey. I'll hang up so you can talk to Jeremy. Holly, I'm so sorry."

"Nothing to be sorry about. He's dead."

"That he is."

Holly hangs up and opens the FaceTime app. It rings and then Jeremy's face appears.

"Hi, cutie!"

"Mommy, Mommy, Mommy!"

"How are you?"

Jeremy smiles as he rocks back and forth with the iPad in his hands. In the distance, Roger is on the phone.

"Sit still, honey. You're making mommy dizzy."

Jeremy settles down a little.

"Have you been a good boy for Grandpa?"

"Grandpa, Grandpa."

"Alright, Jeremy. Mommy should be home soon, O.K.?"

"Mommy home...Mommy home."

"Good night, my sweet prince."

The image changes to Roger.

"He's been really good, but he misses you."

"Not as much as I miss him."

"Well, I've already started asking questions. When do you think you'll be back?"

"If the op goes as planned, we should be back the day after tomorrow."

"Be safe and watch your back."

"I will. Good night, Dad."

"Good night Holly."

Chapter Four

The Seraphina is docked and taking on guests for the party. A man checks their invites before welcoming them on board. Holly and Karla are standing at street level taking it all in.

"You ready for this?" Karla asks.

"I just want to get the job done and go home to Jeremy."

Holly grabs her phone and speed-dials a number.

"Arthur's Dry Cleaning. Ticket number please."

"1956"

"One moment, please."

Kane answers.

"How's it look?"

"Big boat, party people. You know the drill."

"Javi is at the second location awaiting your arrival."

"Roger that." She hangs up and looks toward the boat.

"I meant to ask you. Did Derek get under your skin?" Karla asks.

"Under? He shriveled it."

They head down the steps and join the others lining up. Approaching the front of the line, a crew member addresses them.

"Good evening, ladies. Invites please."

They both pull invite cards out and show them to the man.

"Welcome aboard The Seraphina. Next please."

Holly and Karla begin to mingle.

"There's Heatherwood. How do you wanna play this?" Karla asks.

"Let's wait 'till the speeches are over, then do your thing."

Heatherwood walks over to a hanging bell and starts ringing it.

"Ladies and gentlemen, if I could get your attention. I've gathered you all this evening to introduce Naveet Khan, CEO of WorldRaising Telecomm. Not only is Naveet leading our first female-run company, but she's also the first in our investment group to have a billion-dollar market cap. So with great pleasure, I present, Naveet Khan."

"Thank you, Sam. After serving for the Peace Corps in Latin America and having to wait in line in order to use a satellite phone, I vowed to find a way to offer connectivity to those who don't have it."

"Yep, porn and Candy Crush for all the mud hut kids," Karla whispers.

"I need a drink."

"Lead the way, sister."

Arriving at the bar, Sam Heatherwood sees them and makes his way over.

"Well, I must say I'm honored that you've accepted my invitation. You both look great in the cage, but I must say you look stunning tonight."

"Thank you for having us," Holly says.

"You got some spread here, Mr. Heatherwood."

"Please call me Sam. What are you ladies drinking?"

"I'll have a white wine, please."

"Sparkling water for me," Karla says.

"And I'll have a single malt neat, Jeffrey."

"Very well, sir."

The bartender pours the drinks and places them on the bar. Each person grabs their glass.

"I raise a glass to two formidable women."

Both women raise their glasses in return.

"Thank you, kind sir."

"I hope we can get together later."

Karla smiles. "You can guarantee it."

'Very well then. If you don't mind, I must attend to my other guests." Heatherwood walks off.

"Not too blatant, huh?"

"Me or him?"

Another gentleman approaches the bar.

"Aren't you ladies Holly Hellfire and Karla Krush?"

"Yeah, but we're off duty now."

"Sam told me he was going to have surprise guests tonight. Wow, my son and I are such big fans."

"How old is your son?"

"He's ten. His name is Billy. Do you think I can get a picture with you guys? I think it would make his day."

"His day or yours?" Karla asks.

"Well, both actually."

The man gets in between them and grabs his phone to take the shot.

"Now, can I get one with each of you?"

"That's gonna cost you," Holly says.

How much?

"How much ya got?'

"Seriously?"

"Nah, we're just busting your chops," Karla says.

The man takes shots with both of them and as he leaves, another guy comes up.

"Hello, ladies. Can I get a picture as well?"

"I'm thinking we should set up a carnival photo booth. Charge a hundred bucks a pop.

"Sure, why not," Holly says.

"Was that for me or him?"

"Both of you."

After a few more pictures have been taken, the ladies head off.

"Time to get the lay of the land," Karla says.

"Good idea. That last guy got more than a picture of me." Holly says.

"I'd be sad if they stopped fondling me," Karla says.

Walking around the yacht, Karla stops short.

"Uh oh..."

"What?"

"Two O'clock and bearing down on you."

"Ah, jeez, well maybe we can use this to our advantage."

"You taking one for the team?"

"Do I have a choice?"

Derek approaches with a bewildered look on his face.

"What are you guys doing here?"

"Heatherwood is a fan. He invited us."

"I wasn't aware that he invited you."

"Why would you be?"

"Because Heatherwood is one of our biggest clients."

"So this guy is more important to you than your family?"

"That's not fair, Holly."

"Well, I'm gonna leave you kids alone and find the little girl's room. Play nice now." Karla says as she walks away.

"O.K. I'm going to be civil for a minute and let you explain yourself."

Holly leads Derek off to a quieter place to talk.

Karla mills through the crowd searching for Heatherwood. He's in a conversation when he sees Karla standing alone.

"Would you please excuse me?"

He makes his way over to Karla, who lights up and smiles as he approaches.

"I'd sure like a private tour if you wouldn't mind."

"It would be my pleasure."

"Well, I hope I can add to that."

"Okay then."

Heatherwood offers his arm and they walk off as he points things out.

They appear at the top of the yacht and Heatherwood goes in for a hug and a kiss. Karla responds with a kiss and then pulls back.

"How 'bout we take this party to your stateroom?"

"Let's."

Heatherwood takes Karla's hand and leads her to the main stateroom. The door opens. As Sam and Karla enter, Sam turns and locks the door and dims the lights.

"A drink?"

Karla nods. As Heatherwood turns, Karla eyes the safe set low on the wall.

***

Holly and Derek find a quiet spot near the edge of the vessel looking out into the Gulf of Mexico.

"Beautiful," Derek says.

"The window is closing. Get to it."

He turns to look at her.

"This is pointless. I'm leaving." Holly stands up to go.

"No, wait."

***

Heatherwood flings off his suit jacket and beelines to Karla with two wine glasses in hand.

"Very nice..."

"Yes, you are."

Karla sets her glass down.

"Come over here and close your eyes."

Karla pops a pill in her mouth grabs Heatherwood's face and gives him a French kiss which transfers the pill to Heatherwood.

"This is going to heighten the experience."

She breaks the kiss and tells him to keep his eyes closed as she unbuckles his pants.

***

Holly is standing with her arms crossed, glowering down at Derek.

"Things have gotten so much more complicated than they were in Afghanistan.

"And?"

"Look, there's moles everywhere. The CIA, NSA, FBI, every private contractor, our allies, enemies. No one's sure who they can trust anymore."

"What does this have to do with abandoning your family?"

"I'm in the middle of it all. It's something big..."

***

Karla takes a sip of her wine and then flashes Sam a smile. He sweats and tries to conceal the discomfort on his face.

"Everything all right, Sam?"

"I don't feel too good."

"Don't worry, it gets better."

He opens his eyes wide as his breathing becomes labored.

"What's wrong, Sammy seasick?"

Heatherwood grabs his throat as Karla knocks him to his knees. She pulls an Epi-Pen from her clutch and shows it to him.

"You want me to save you?"

Heatherwood nods yes and tries to grab the Epi-Pen from her.

"Not so fast. Open the safe and give me the hard drive or Sammy doesn't get to see Jake, Harry, Allison, and Melissa. And what about that wife of yours getting everything you own? The safe, Sam. Time's ticking and your ticker won't last without this."

Heatherwood crawls over to the safe, struggles to open it, and does so before he collapses. Karla reaches in, takes the drive, puts it in a waterproof bag, and slips it into her clutch. She gets up, stabs Heatherwood with the Epi-Pen, and heads out of the stateroom.

She grabs her phone and sends a text to Javi:

Got it, do it.

＊

Holly shakes her head and rolls her eyes.

"You're just rambling now. Stop being so cryptic. I'm a big girl. Whatever it is, just come out and say it."

"I can't. Just know that my new identity protects our son. All my loved ones would be in danger 24-7. That's why I can't be tied to any of you."

A small explosion is heard as the cabin fills with smoke. People run in the opposite direction.

Derek breaks away from Holly and sprints toward the disturbance.

Holly scans the crowd for Karla, as Karla gives the high sign and points to the rear of the boat. They both meet at the fantail, shrug off their dresses, revealing one-piece bathing suits, and dive off the boat.

As Holly and Karla submerge, two frogmen with propelled units grab each one, put scuba masks on them, and head off.

Tommy hears the commotion on board The Seraphina. He grabs binoculars and sees Holly and Karla diving off the fantail.

Moments later, Tommy hoists Holly and Karla aboard a Zodiac boat along with the two frogmen.

"Thanks, Tommy."

"Yeah, let's get the hell out of here and get smashed."

"Sounds good to me."

"Hiya, boys. My name's Karla. Thanks for fishing us out."

The Zodiac peels off and heads for safety. They all dig into their duffels and pull out street clothes. The frogmen peel off their wet suits and get changed. The girls towel off and throw on dark sweats.

Suddenly, the sound of a jet ski coming towards them gets louder.

"We got company."

One of the frogmen pulls HK 416 assault rifles from the duffels and tosses them to Holly, Karla, and his partner. They all get low and take a bead on the incoming target.

The jet ski rider fires two phosphorus rounds into the air lighting up the sky. They see the target clearly and begin to lay down fire. The jet ski rider returns with automatic fire. Tommy takes evasive maneuvers. As it gets closer, the jet ski slows and stops dead in the water as smoke billows from the engine.

"I think he's down."

The zodiac speeds off as the phosphorus dies.

★ ★ ★

On board the Seraphina, Sam is slumped in a chair, tie askew and collar wide open as he downs a bottle of water. Derek paces back and forth. He smashes a mirror with his fist.

"You had specific instructions to inform us of every single person who was stepping foot on this vessel."

"But they're just MMA fighters. Minor celebrities. I couldn't see the harm in..."

"You pay us to see. We're your eyes. Holly and her friends aren't just some cute faces looking for a good time."

Derek picks up a wine glass and throws it across the room. It shatters. Sam flinches.

"They're mercenaries for hire and your libido just let them run off with all that info on the drive."

"Wherever I turn, I'm running into mercenaries and deep-state actors. Jesus, does this crap ever end? Heatherwood says.

"That's why we're here. And now, so are they. They're good, but I don't think they realize what they're in for."

"How good?"

"Holly's crafty, intelligent, and a fighter but also arrogant and a little reckless. I'm guessing her new team is the same way. Don't worry. We'll get the drive back."

He gets on his phone and storms off.

***

As the Zodiac boat comes ashore, the frogmen jump off and secure it so that Holly and Karla can exit to a laundry delivery truck. One of the frogmen slaps the side of the truck and the back door rolls up.

A man helps Holly and Karla up and into two large laundry carts secured to the wall, then covers them with piles of bedsheets.

The man jumps down and pulls the door along with him, gets behind the wheel, and pulls away.

* * *

Derek is dockside pacing back and forth as he's on the phone.

"I just sent you their pictures. Get out there and find them."

The laundry truck backs into the loading dock of a downtown hotel. Two men exit. One rolls up the door and the other gets in and unstraps the laundry carts.   Both men wheel the carts out and enter the bowels of the hotel.

A large man in a suit approaches the hotel reception area and pulls out his phone.

"Good evening, sir. Welcome to the Marina Side Hilton. How can I help you?"

"Have you seen or checked in either of these two women?"

"I have not, but one of our associates may have. I can check if you wouldn't mind waiting."

The man grumbles, turns heads over to the lounge area, and grabs a seat where he's able to watch who's coming and going.

The 5th floor elevator bell dings and two room service carts are wheeled out to room 508. One of the men knocks on the door.

"Room service."

The door opens and Javi Ordonez steps aside as the carts enter the suite.

Javi tips the men and closes the door behind them.”

“Honey, room service is here.”

From under one of the carts a high-pitched voice says:

“O.K. Javi.”

Holly and Karla emerge from under the carts, stand up and stretch.

“I don't know about you, but I feel like a pretzel,” Karla says.

“Would you settle for a club sandwich instead?” Javi says.

“Hold mine. I need a shower first.” Holly says as she heads to the bathroom.

“Not me. I'm starved.”

"Ah, you got something for me maybe?" Javi says.

Karla reaches behind her and hands Javi the drive.

"Here ya go kid."

"Thanks, let me boot it up and see what we've got."

Javi boots up the drive. As he's scanning the contents he reacts.

"Oh boy."

"What?"

"I gotta call Arty and we gotta get outta here."

"Can I finish eating first?"

Javi grabs his phone and speed-dials.

"Arthur's Dry Cleaning. Ticket number please."

"1978."

"One moment, please."

"Javi."

"They're in and O.K."

"Great, and the drive?"

"Just did a cursory scan and I saw some interesting files definitely not related to the supercollider project."

"Really?"

"I want to encrypt them and send them over. I also suggest you escalate the extrication plans so we're out of here within the hour."

"Call you back."

At a table in the back of a biker bar, Tommy, the two frogmen, and the laundry guys sit around the table drinking beers.

"Thanks for helping out tonight, fellas."

"I enjoyed the rec, plus that brunette was just my style."

"What's her story, Tommy?"

"She's feisty. Can kick any guy's ass and I protect her like she's my little sister."

Tommy gets a text and sends a quick reply.

"Seems we pissed off a few people."

"Then it was a good op in my book."

"They don't know you guys, but the three of us are tagged."

"So what do you need us to do?"

"Let me settle up the tab and then we'll shove off and talk in the car."

An armored car rolls up and backs into the loading dock. The passenger gets out and goes up to the loading dock and into the hotel.

The driver gets out and walks around to the front entrance.

The driver enters and scans the lobby area as he approaches the main desk.

"Good evening, sir. Welcome to the Marina Side Hilton. How can I help you?"

"I'd like to settle my bill. I'm checking out."

"Room number, please."

"508."

The receptionist pulls up the invoice and the driver hands over a credit card. The driver turns and re-scans the lobby. He catches the large man's glance at him just before the man ducks his head into a newspaper.

The receptionist hands back the card and invoice.

"Here you go, sir. Enjoy your night."

"You too. Good night now."

The driver exits and grabs his phone, speed dialing a number.

"Yeah, I made one guy about 5' 10", 280 in the lobby. How long 'till load out?"

The driver listens and replies.

"O.K. I'm on my way."

The driver approaches the loading dock and sees two men in suits exiting from the back seat of a black Chevy Suburban and crossing the street on a diagonal. He senses trouble walks past the loading dock and doubles back across the street.

One man heads towards the lobby and the other enters the loading dock area.

The man checks the cab of the armored car and a bread delivery truck that is backed into the loading dock. Seeing they're empty, he scans the area again, and then enters the hotel.

The driver casually walks back to the loading dock as the bread delivery driver jumps in his truck.

The armored truck driver gets in and both vehicles pull out and go in separate directions.

Two men in the Suburban watch the loading dock as both vehicles depart.

"That armored truck driver looked a little hinky. You think that's them in there?"

"Only one way to find out."

The Suburban pulls out and follows the armored car.

As the Bread Delivery driver makes his way through town, Holly, Karla, and Javi are in the back feasting on pastries.

"Ya got any coffee up there to go with these pastries?"

"Nah, sorry, we grabbed this 'cause it was convenient."

The armored car stops at a light. The suburban is a few car lengths behind.

The light turns green and both vehicles proceed.

"We need confirmation now. You got your credentials, right?"

The passenger gives a thumbs-up as he listens to his earpiece.

"About to pull the armored car over. Stand by."

As the armored car rolls ahead, the Suburban pulls out and cuts it off. Two motorcycles also speed up to it. The passenger jumps out and approaches the armored car on the driver's side. He quickly flashes some sort of badge without the driver getting a good look.

"There's a couple of high-priority suspects in the area. We have to check the back of your truck. We can do this the easy way or the hard way."

He motions to the two motorcyclists. They open their jackets revealing machine guns. The driver slowly gets out, arms raised.

"Move faster."

Suit 2 pushes him to the back of the armored car. The driver opens the back doors. It's empty.

"Gimme your phone."

The driver hands it over. The man drops it on the ground and smashes it to pieces with his boot heel. He turns and heads back to the Suburban, talking into his earpiece.

"Find that bread truck and send me the coordinates."

The motorcycles and the Suburban U-turn and speed off.

The delivery driver eats a bagel as he's driving. A white van pulls out from a side street and sits in the middle of the road.

The driver's side window rolls down and the van driver fires a shot into the bread truck windshield. The delivery driver is hit in the arm and drops the bagel. The truck swerves, just missing the van. Javi, Holly, and Karla tumble around in the back. Holly takes out her gun and crawls to the front of the truck.

"Javi, call Tommy."

"Tommy, it's an ambush. I'm sending our coordinates."

The white van trails behind the truck. Holly takes her jacket off makes a tourniquet out of the sleeve and wraps it around the driver's arm. She switches spots with him and takes the wheel.

Gunshots pierce the back door. Javi flattens himself against the wall. Karla pops open the back door and starts shooting at the white van. An incoming bullet hits Javi's laptop. Karla plugs the driver right between the eyes and the van swerves and crashes into parked cars.

The motorcycles roar down the street past the crashing van as the riders fire at the back of the truck.

Karla jumps and dives away from the door behind some racks of baked goods in the truck. She pushes two racks off the back as rounds continue to hit the truck. One of the shots blows out a back tire.

The racks tumble in the road. One motorcycle crashes into a rack and dumps the rider. The other motorcyclist dodges the rack but loses control and crashes into a parked car.

"Guess they didn't like jelly doughnuts," Karla says.

The Suburban turns from a side street and pulls alongside. Karla grabs onto the door, swings out, and fires at the Suburban. The Suburban passenger shoots out both driver's side tires. Sparks fly as the rims dig against the road.

Holly tries to keep control. Karla swings herself back in. The truck swerves out of control.

"Hold on," Holly yells.

The delivery truck overturns and slides across the pavement. The men in the Suburban jump out and run at the downed van with guns drawn.

Everyone in the truck is disoriented.

The first guy rips open the delivery truck's back door. A shot is fired and he drops. The other guy turns around and sees Tommy coming out of an SUV and firing at him. The two men briefly exchange fire.

"Hey," Karla says to the guy.

He turns and sees a bloodied Karla and Holly with guns drawn on him.

He turns back to Tommy, who winks and smiles.

The man turns back to Holly and Karla then looks down at his gun. He starts to raise his hands in surrender but quickly puts the gun to his head and fires.

* * *

Tommy's SUV roars onto the tarmac, circles around, and stops at a jet that is powered up and ready to go. Holly, Karla, and Javi exit the SUV and head up the stairs to the jet.

Tommy gets out and helps the delivery truck driver get behind the wheel.

"Hey, man. Sorry, you had to take a round."

"Not the first time, Tommy."

"Rocco's on his way. Just pull beyond the gate and let him drive. He'll get that fixed for you."

"We're here for ya, Tommy. You call, we haul."

"Without a doubt, brother. Without a doubt."

Tommy slaps the hood and the driver pulls out as Tommy heads up into the jet. The Flight Attendant pulls the door up and minutes later, the jet taxis out and takes off.

Holly, Javi, and Tommy sit back quietly taking it all in. Karla digs in her bag for her meds. She brings them up popping two in her mouth and drowning them with a bottle of water.

"Hittin' the Pez dispenser again, huh?" Holly says.

"Yeah, my shoulder is screaming. That cement mixer move didn't do me any good."

"How 'bout you, Javi? How are you holding up?"

"I'm really pissed that they took out my laptop."

"That can be replaced."

"Tommy, as always, thanks for the support, and please thank your buds. We couldn't have done this without them." Holly says.

"Will do, but I think they enjoyed it a little too."

Artemis Kane rings through on the large screen monitor attached to the bulkhead.

"Hi, kids."

"Hi, Daddy!" they all say in unison.

"Sit rep please."

"We got a little banged up after we met up with our welcoming party," Holly says.

"That was definitely an E-ticket ride. Thanks for the bread truck and pastries, Arty."

"Wasn't me. Thank Tommy and his friends for that one."

"I think that little dustup was the start of some blowback from my risen from the dead ex-husband."

"Yeah, I heard something about that."

"We found out they had someone in the lobby of the hotel and as we were leaving, and then more of them showed up," Tommy says.

"Holly, were you able to get anything out of him on the boat?"

"No specifics about his post-mortem life. He was being very vague and semi-apologetic."

"So the only thing we know for sure is that he's tied into Heatherwood."

The Commander is pulling some strings to get to the bottom of it, so I suggest you give him a shout but don't go empty-handed. He says you owe him a bottle of Macallan." Holly says.

"If he sheds some light on Derek's new life, then I'll come bearing a case of Macallan."

"Let me know when you do that. I'll come bearing straws." Karla says.

"Javi, did the drive survive the exfil?

"Yeah, good thing it was solid state."

"I took a look at those encrypted files you sent over."

"What was on them?" Holly says.

"Another can of worms for us to deal with."

Chapter Five

In a run-down neighborhood, a few cars are parked in an unkempt parking lot of a laundromat. Tommy's loud Harley pulls in. He carries a small laundry bag. Tommy walks in and drops the bag on the counter.

A laundromat employee comes from behind the racks of dry cleaning. Tommy nods, looks around, then steps behind the counter.

The employee takes the laundry bag and buzzes Tommy into a door behind the rack of dry-cleaned clothes that leads to a dark stairway.

A steel door is against the far wall of the basement. Tommy is buzzed in again into a clean, high-tech command center.

Artemis, Javi, Holly, and Karla sit around a conference table.

"So, do either of you have any matches coming up that I should know about?" Kane asks.

"I don't have anything scheduled for the rest of the month," Holly says.

They've been trying to get us to do something, but my shoulder is acting up, so I need to hold off for a while." Karla says.

Tommy walks in and takes a seat at the table.

"Hey, Tommy."

"So what kind of goodies did we get?"

"There's a treasure trove of stuff here. Too early to say for sure what else we've found."

"I'm still decrypting some of it and going through the rest. There are a lot of files here. Some of them are written in code, so we'll have to crack that in order to figure out what's really on them." Javi says.

"The drive was returned, minus those extra files, to a very appreciative client. He wired the balance, so disbursements have been made to each of your offshore accounts." Kane says.

"Cha ching!" Karla says.

Outside the Laundry, an SUV with tinted windows pulls up across the street. The window rolls down a bit. A camera lens peeks out the driver-side window. After a couple of pictures are taken, the window rolls up and the SUV pulls away.

Kane walks around the table and hands each person a file folder.

"A list of names."

"Of who?" Tommy asks.

"Derek Prince is one of them. I've searched the other names listed and found some records and IDs with corresponding pictures." Javi says.

"Aliases, undercover IDs..." Tommy says.

"I know this name, Ted Carmine, formerly of Blackwater. Also allegedly MIA in Afghanistan." Holly says.

"It could be current and former agents from several different agencies and programs. I don't know what type of hornet's nest we stumbled upon. I'll have to step lightly as I reach out and try to connect the dots."

"These last pages are all travel logs. Do they tie to these guys?" Karla asks.

"I've already run every name and there's no obvious connection between them and these travel dates," Javi says.

"So, people of interest they were surveilling?" Tommy asks.

Karla recites the list. "Libya, Bahrain, Azerbaijan, Sudan, Angola, Chad."

"All dictatorships. Some our government openly supports, others they don't.

All either have various terrorist ties, valuable natural resources, or both." Holly says.

"Yes, well this is something to mull over but I'm expecting a more immediate job in the next few days. I'll keep you posted."

They all get up, except Javi, who's still focused on his computer. Kane collects the files.

Tommy, Karla, and Holly head up the stairs. Karla pulls out her vitamin bottle, quickly tosses a pill in her mouth, and swallows it dry.

"You and your vitamins," Tommy says.

"That's my lunch."

Jeremy bounces up and down on a small indoor trampoline, flapping his hands, as he looks out the front picture window.

From the front seat view of a car, Jeremy is seen jumping on the trampoline.

The sound of a muscle car approaching gets louder as Holly's Black Shelby Cobra turns the corner, comes down the street, and turns into the driveway.

She exits the car and stops in front of the window waving to Jeremy, who beams and mouths the words Mommy...Mommy!

The door opens and Holly runs over to Jeremy and lifts him off the trampoline.

"How are you, my prince? I missed you so much."

"Mommy home...mommy home."

"Yeah, sweetie. Mommy's home."

Holly's father enters the living room.

"Hey, Dad."

"How did it go?"

Holly is still holding Jeremy in her arms.

"Let's just say we have a lot to talk about."

Afterword

Thanks for your support and for taking time out of your day to read "KAOS."

Your support and patronage of all things generated by Testaforte Entertainment is greatly appreciated.

I'd also be remiss in my marketing efforts if I didn't graciously ask you for reviews of any products you buy from us.

As an independent publisher, your support means so much to me.

If you can spare 60 seconds, seeing your honest feedback as a review does wonders for me and future readers.

Thank you in advance, all the best, and be well,

Nicky.

About the Author

Nicky Testaforte is a prolific author known for his diverse range of literary works spanning multiple genres. His passion for writing and dedication to crafting engaging and informative content has resulted in a remarkable body of work that has captured the hearts and minds of readers of all ages.

One of his most notable accomplishments is the 10-book Early Enrichment Series designed to stimulate young minds. The goal is to enrich Fine Motor Skills, Encourage Focus, and Nurture Creativity Through Reading, Writing and Coloring.

All of his books are available on Amazon through http://www.testafortebooks.com

He is also a Voice Actor and Audio Editor. Check out his demos at:
http://www.soundcloud.com/nickytestaforte/sets

Adult Titles By Testaforte Books

Nicky Testaforte's
Tales of a
NEW YORK
LIMO DRIVER
Sex, Excess & Stupidity On Four Wheels
BEST SELLER
PARENTAL
ADVISORY
EXPLICIT CONTENT

Excerpt from "Tales of a New York Limo Driver"

A driver gets to the client's home and backs into his driveway. He pops the trunk and checks his mirrors to see if the client is coming.

The client comes out and waves to the driver as if to say "It's O.K., I've got it" as he's putting his bags in the trunk and closing it. The client goes around to the right rear door, opens it, and realizes that he's forgotten something.

He closes the door, starts walking back to the house, and the driver takes off without him.

The client goes inside to retrieve what he forgot and calls the limo company.

"Hi, this is Mr. Jones. Your driver just pulled away from my house with my luggage in the car and left me behind."

The dispatcher gets the driver on the radio, asks him where he is, and then says:

"OK stupid, make a U-turn and go back and get your client."

What a friggin' idiot.

Nicky Testaforte's
EXACTING RETRIBUTION
Revenge Done Right

Excerpt from "Exacting Retribution"

A 1965 Chevy Impala with its lights off cruises slowly up a dimly lit suburban tree-lined street. Inside, two men dressed in black are scanning the street looking for a specific address.

"Are you sure this is the place?" the driver says.

"Yes, I'm sure. Ricky said it was this one. Pull over."

The two men exit the car, quietly closing the doors. One has a crowbar, the other a shotgun. They walk up the path to the house.

A ten-year-old boy is woken by the sound of glass breaking and people entering the house. He jumps from his bed and heads for the safety of his closet, covered by a pile of stuffed animals.

Footsteps get louder as they climb the stairs to the second floor. The voices get louder, he hears heavy footsteps coming closer to him. The closet door is pulled open and the door jamb is filled with the backlit image of a very large man, who stands there silently.

"Hey man, get down here. Let's go."

The man exits, leaving the closet door open. The boy hears the men yelling.

"Where's the safe? We know it's here. Don't lie to me bitch."

"What safe, I have no idea what you are talking about!" His Mother screams.

The boy hears a loud bang. The boy is frightened and hides deeper in the pile of stuffed animals. The men run down the hall, head downstairs and exit the house slamming the door.

The boy waits cautiously until the house is quiet again. He emerges from under the stuffed animals and walks out into the hallway down toward his brother's room.

His brother is blankly staring back at him, covered in blood. The boy backs out of the room and runs down the hallway to his parents' room. He trips over his dead father lying face down just inside the doorway. The boy raises himself to see the horror of a blood-spattered wall and his mother motionless below it.

The front door opens as the boy runs barefoot from his house. Mouth wide open, unable to scream, tears streaming down his face and blood all over his dinosaur pajamas.

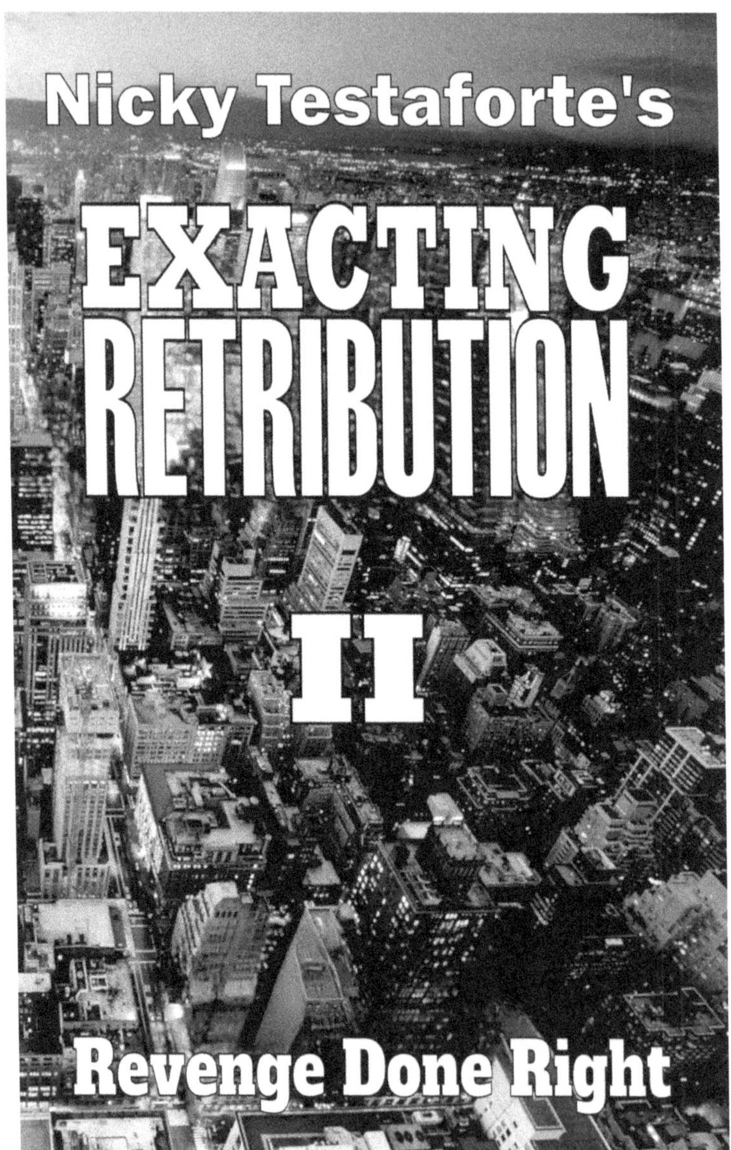

Nicky Testaforte's
EXACTING RETRIBUTION
II
Revenge Done Right

Excerpt from "Exacting Retribution II"

"This is Sam Vargas; do you remember me?"

"Of course, I do. How are things, Sam?" JD Kendall says

"Very well sir, but one of my associates is in the market for your services.

"Referrals are always nice."

"What would be the best way to get you background on her project?"

"A messenger will pick up a package addressed to Mr. Ford at your company's front desk. Call me when it's ready."

"Sounds good, I'll be in touch. Thank you, sir."

"Glad to be of service."

Days later, seated in the outer office of JD's playroom are former Army Ranger Roy Ingram and Private Detective Vic Valrello. JD finishes a conversation on his cell and kicks off a planning meeting.

"Okay boys, our latest piece of shit is Kenny Mastrantonio. He started his career in medicine as a dentist. All went well until he got hit with a malpractice suit, lost his license, and began selling regenerated flesh to burn centers."

Nicky Testaforte's
JUSTIFIED
RETRIBUTION
Vengeance Is Mine

Excerpt from "Justified Retribution"

The unlocked door opens, Ali listens for a second and then steps inside protected by the loud music playing. She moves stealthily through the first floor towards the source of the music.

Seated at his computer with his back to the door of his office, Paul Avery is air drumming to Phil Collins's "In the Air Tonight." Ali quickly moves in putting her right arm around his throat and her left hand over his mouth. Avery begins to fight until Ali whispers in his ear:

"Calm down or I'll snap your neck and kill you right here. You will listen clearly and do as I say. Do you understand?"

Avery stunned by her strength and swiftness shakes his head yes. Taking her hand off his mouth she grabs his hand and pulls his arm behind his back and raises him off the chair, putting pressure on his throat.

"Who are you? If you want money, I'll get it for you, just don't hurt me."

"Shut up and walk towards the garage. Try anything stupid, and I'll drop you right where you stand."

Avery starts walking and then tries to break loose. Ali loosens up enough to let Avery break free, then plants a high kick to his thigh which breaks a bone, dropping Avery screaming in pain on the floor.

"Thought you could break loose huh? Well dipshit, here's a news flash. I let you go, so I could kick your ass."

Ali steps on his broken leg putting pressure on it. Avery screams.

"Oh, does that hurt tough guy?"

Ali then gives him a swift kick to the stomach.

"Digest that, I'll be right back."

Ali goes to the garage for supplies. As Avery groans, there are noises coming from the garage. Ali returns with a weightlifter's belt. She threads it over his chest and under his arms and begins dragging him to the garage.

Avery is screaming:

" Who are you and what do you want?"

"Shut up asshole, I can't hear the music."

Three Retribution Books for the Price of Two!

Nicky Testaforte's
RETRIBUTION THRILLER COLLECTION
Exacting Retribution
Exacting Retribution II
Justified Retribution
Revenge Done Right

Nicky Testaforte's
GRANTED
This Ride Could Be
Life Changing...

Excerpt from "Granted"

"Good evening, ladies. My name is Sandro. Where are you headed?"

"Hello, Sandro. I'm Callie and this is my daughter, Carissa. We're going to Grand Central."

"Grand Central, it is. The 9/11 memorial is unforgettable, isn't it?"

"Sure is."

"This your first visit here?"

"Yes."

"9/11, was a tragic day for all of us."

"Especially my daughter and I."

"Did you lose someone?"

"I lost my husband and Carissa lost her father."

"I'm so sorry. My condolences."

"Thank you. It's taken us a long time to muster up the courage to come here."

"I can only imagine."

"My husband was a Pastry Chef at Windows on the World. He went in early that morning to prepare for a lunch meeting and... well this visit was cathartic for me as much as it was for my daughter. She never knew her father. Carissa was born six months after we lost him."

"I'm so sorry."

"It's been difficult to say the least. So, we take it one day at a time. Are you all right, Carissa?"

"I feel really sad for everyone who lost someone that day."

"Are you with me, sir?"

"Yes Sandro. Hello, ladies. My name is Paul Grant. It's a pleasure to meet you."

"Who's that, Sandro?"

"That's my boss. You should listen to what he has to say."

"Your story has moved me tremendously. So, first off, I'd like Sandro to drive you and your daughter straight home tonight."

"Oh, no, that's all right. To tell you the truth, we just have enough money for the train ride home."

"We understand your hesitation at the gesture. It's your first time in the city on Christmas Eve, and then some Cab Driver and a disembodied voice offer you a ride home. I know it's strange, but we insist!"

"That's very nice of you."

"You're welcome... I'm sorry, but I didn't catch your last name."

"Vincent, but please call me, Callie. And this is my daughter Carissa."

"Very well, then. Callie and Carissa. I've decided to break with tradition this evening. My financial advisor, Valerie Purcell, will present my gift to you and Carissa at your home tomorrow."

"You're already driving us home. That's more than enough. And you have gifts for us as well? It's so unusual. I don't know what to say."

"Thanks aren't necessary. And with that, I must attend to a pressing matter. It's been a pleasure meeting both of you. Sandro will take things from here. Good night and Merry Christmas!"

"Merry Christmas Mr. Grant."

Callie then tries to process what's happened.

Nicky Testaforte's
The Driver
A Rideshare Serial Killer Story

Excerpt from "The Driver"

Barb sees her next passenger standing on the corner. She turns the radio down and pulls up to the client. Upset, the passenger gets in and sighs.

"What took you so long? I've been standing out here for fifteen minutes waiting for you."

"Well, I gotcha now."

"I hope you're not one of those females that doesn't know how to drive."

"You think I don't know how to drive?"

She floors it and takes a corner so fast that he has to hold on to the armrest.

"All right, all right. Please, I want to get home in one piece."

Barb laughs as the glass divider rolls up and the cabin fills with smoke. The passenger is banging on the divider and Barb responds by giving him the finger.

The black Camry makes a turn and stops next to a park bench. Barb gets out, opens the rear passenger door, and drags the unconscious man onto the park bench. He looks like he's sleeping off a bender.

Barb gets back into the Camry and heads home. Julio, the Rideshare driver is restrained in a chair. Barb emerges from the shadows of the darkened basement and walks in front of an elevated blood-stained table with meat cleavers and power saws.

"Why are you doing this, please let me go!"

"You are here to play a part. Have you ever considered dabbling in TV, movies, or even Broadway?"

"Untie me you sick bitch."

"Not just yet, but I will. Then you're going to be famous."

Barb gags Julio with a wet rag, then places a modified motorcycle helmet onto his head, blocking sound and vision.

Barb walks to the stairs, turns, and looks back without emotion. She goes upstairs and shuts the lights off in the basement. Barb enters the kitchen and encounters her mother glowering at her.

"What the hell were you doing down there? It's after 12 Noon and I need my lunch."

"Sorry, I had to run to the store, we ran out of rat poison for your stew."

"I rue the day you were born Barbara. You've been nothing but trouble for me."

NICKY TESTAFORTE'S

KAOS

KICK ASS
OPERATIVES
SERVICE

Excerpt from "K.A.O.S."

Karla looks on as the trainer finishes tending to Holly's cut. Holly takes out her phone and dials a number.

"Hey honey, It's mommy. Calling to say I love you and miss you. I'll see you soon okay, buddy?"

Karla sees the fight doctor turn down a hallway. She follows him. The doctor looks around somewhat nervously as Karla approaches. Karla is carefree and smiling.

"Eh...What's up, doc?"

"You know, this is getting increasingly difficult for me and risky to my reputation."

"Aw, my hero."

"Enough, Karla. Here, ten milligram oxy is all I could get."

"Ten? Last time it was twenty and I told you that crap gives me horror show nightmares and side effects."

"So you don't want them?"

"Did I say that? I'm not paying extra for a weaker pill."

"More risk, same price."

"You realize I could beat the crap out of you and just take them?"

"I don't dispute that. If those are the thoughts going through your head, then you most definitely have a problem."

"It's a joke, doc."

Karla enters the bathroom and looks in the mirror. She shakes out her right shoulder and then takes the pill bottle out. She tosses two pills in her mouth, swallowing them dry.

She pulls a vitamin bottle out of her purse. She dumps the pills in, throws the pill bottle into the trash, and exits the bathroom.

As Karla comes out of the bathroom, Holly walks toward her with a towel over her head.

"Yo, towel head!

"Not now, sister. I need a fistful of painkillers and a long hot shower."

Just as Karla is about to respond, her phone rings.

"It's Kane."

Holly grabs the phone from Karla and puts it on speaker.

"Who's this?"

"Very funny. I hope you've saved up your strength and didn't get too beat up."

"She looked beat up before she got into the ring."

Holly elbows Karla in the ribs.

"Did ya call just to chat, 'cause I'd like to stand under a hot shower till the water runs out?"

"If you did that, you'd melt like a candle."

Karla sways and gets smaller.

"I'm melting, I'm melting."

"Ladies, we've got a job. Go home and pack a bag. You're going to Texas."

"For barbecue?"

"No wonder you're so fat…"

"Settle down, ladies. I suggest you pack a couple of slinky dresses along with your rip stops."

"Ooh, a swanky job. Cool."

"The jet leaves Teterboro tomorrow at 9 AM. Don't be late."

"Are ya sure she has to come?"

"Hey!

"Oh, this one requires both of your specific charms."

"She doesn't have any charms."

"Enough sparring, ladies. Times ticking and Texas calls. Say goodbye."

Karla covers Holly's mouth and grabs the phone from her hands. Holly breaks loose, comes behind Karla, and puts a choke hold on her

Karla takes a breath and says: "Bye, Arty!"

Nicky Testaforte's

Black Book

of

50 Original Dark Drama and Comedy Scenes For Actors

Vol. 1

Excerpt from "Black Book"

G-Ro Investigations

<u>ROSALIE</u>

Is your significant other doin' the horizontal nasty with someone other than you?

<u>GINO</u>

You wanna prove that somebody's dirty, but you just don't know how?

<u>RO & GINO</u>

Welcome to G-Ro Investigations

<u>ROSALIE</u>

Private dicks if you will.

<u>GINO</u>

We'll set loose our network of trusted associates to get you what you need.

<u>ROSALIE</u>

You want photos, video? If ya want a Polaroid, we can get that too. Can we?

<u>GINO</u>

I guess so.

<u>ROSALIE</u>

No matta what you want found out, we'll found it for ya.

<u>GINO</u>

G-Ro Investigations

(Gino is holding up a magnifying glass and Rosalie, paper maps.)

<u>GINO</u>

We got the tools…

<u>ROSALIE</u>

…as long as you got the money.

GINO

Lots of it!

ROSALIE

2nd floor just above McNulty's bar. Knock four times so we know it's you. And G, don't forget yours is private. You even think of taking that thing elsewhere, I'll get the poultry scissors and cut that chicken right off. Snip, snip

GINO

Hey!

Nicky Testaforte's
TV &
MUSIC
TRIVIA
60s to 90s
OVER 700 MULTIPLE CHOICE TV
& MUSIC QUESTIONS FOR TRIVIA
NIGHTS AT HOME OR AT THE BAR

The Questions

Only two of the following are both band names and car companies. Which one isn't?

REO Speedwagon

Tesla

Pantera

Which "Olympic Sport" song did Ronnie James Dio record?

Holy Diver

Jump

Run Runaway

Kids Titles By Testaforte Books

Goals of the Early Enrichment Series:

Improve Fine Motor Skills, Encourage Focus, and Nurture Creativity Through Reading, Writing, and Coloring

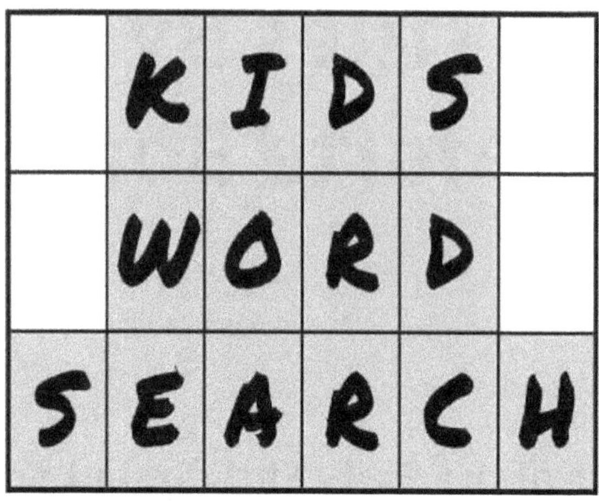

100+ Diverse Categories With Over 10 Clues Per Grid That Will Challenge Young Minds

Nicky Testaforte

NICKY TESTAFORTE'S
EARLY ENRICHMENT SERIES

ALPHABET TRACING

Book One

NICKY TESTAFORTE'S
EARLY ENRICHMENT SERIES

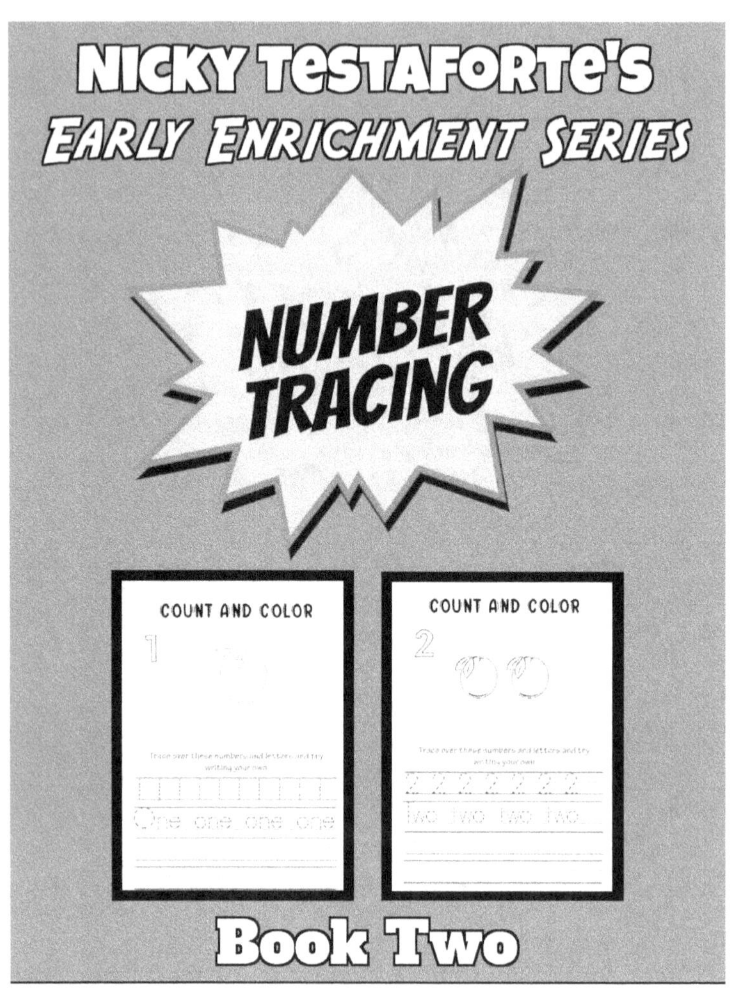

Book Two

NICKY TESTAFORTE'S
EARLY ENRICHMENT SERIES

Book Three

NICKY TESTAFORTE'S
EARLY ENRICHMENT SERIES

CREATIVE COLORING

Book Four

NICKY TESTAFORTE'S
EARLY ENRICHMENT SERIES

Book Five

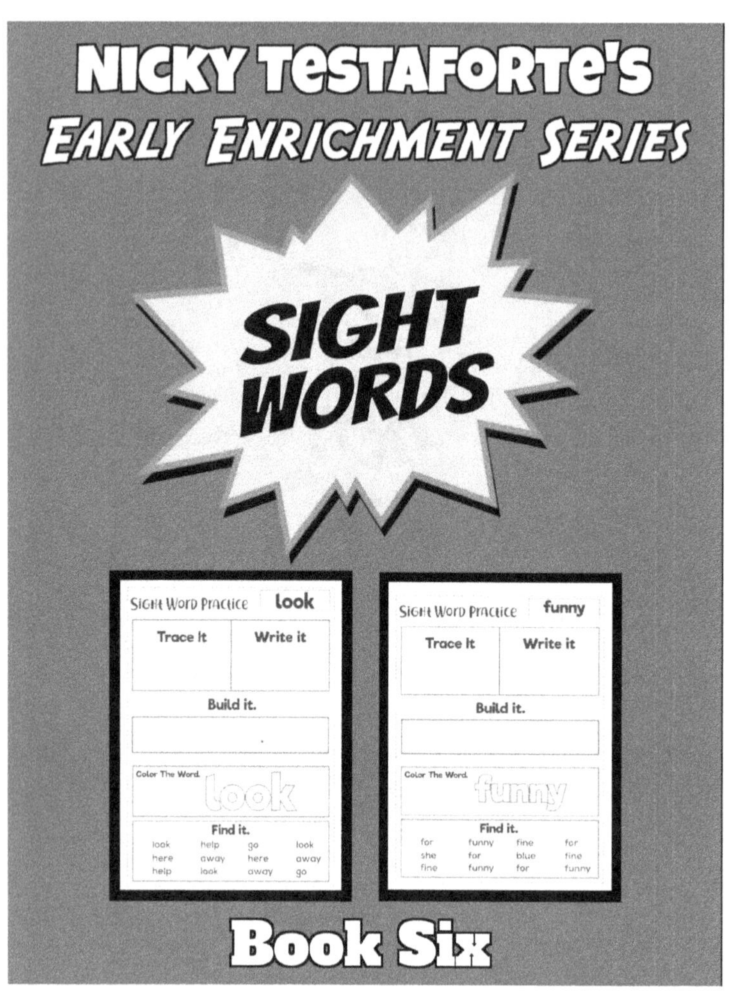
NICKY TESTAFORTE'S
EARLY ENRICHMENT SERIES
SIGHT WORDS
Sight Word Practice   look
Trace It   Write it
Build it.
Color The Word.   look
Find it.
look   help   go   look
here   away   here   away
help   look   away   go
Sight Word Practice   funny
Trace It   Write it
Build it.
Color The Word.   funny
Find it.
for   funny   fine   for
she   for   blue   fine
fine   funny   for   funny
Book Six

NICKY TESTAFORTE'S
EARLY ENRICHMENT SERIES

Book Seven

NICKY TESTAFORTE'S
EARLY ENRICHMENT SERIES

Book Eight

NICKY TESTAFORTE'S
EARLY ENRICHMENT SERIES

MIX OF THINGS

Book Nine

NICKY TESTAFORTE'S
EARLY ENRICHMENT SERIES

Book Ten

NICKY TESTAFORTE'S
EARLY ENRICHMENT SERIES
PRESENTS THE:

HUMONGOUS
BOOK OF
LEARNING

11 BOOKS IN ONE!

**492 Challenging Worksheets From
The Early Enrichment Series
Plus As An Added Bonus:
100 Page Kids Word Search**

www.testafortebooks.com